Chapter Zero: Prologue; The Suffering of Suburbia

Suffering manifests when the modernity of suburbia fractures. I'm sure some famous dead person said this. If not, maybe it will appear on my notable quotes page when I'm dead.

Mine cracked a week ago like a hammer to the face.

What started as just another repetitious weekday unraveled rapidly into dysfunction.

My sister and I woke up with no skin. There would be no issue if it was just the layer that falls off in your sleep, but we looked like an anatomy model, like that one titan from Attack on Titan.

The media loved it; they wrote a shit ton of articles. My favorite is twin-track superstars Stephen and Sarah O'Leary caught with their skin down. A nursery rhyme was also made, but I would just ruin it if I repeated such magnificence.

Everything that followed our skinning was outrageous. It was as if the slow leak in our society finally stopped. The result: our collective corpse being cannibalized by horrid events.

Chapter One: A Nursery Rhyme is Just an Early Method of Indoctrination

The skinless twins!

The skinless twins!

Don't let them touch you

or they will steal your skin.

The skinless twins!

The skinless twins!

Don't let them touch you

or the devil wins.

The skinless twins!

The skinless twins!

Woe is them.

Our stares,

they sting.

Chapter Two: Roc Harde A.M.

In a rent-controlled studio basement located on the former swamplands of Country Club, two boys, with a combined year total of thirty-two, sit side by side at a black wooden coffee table. With all sorts of radio broadcasting equipment in front of them, stuff I wouldn't know how to describe, they get ready for their daily morning broadcast. Nobody knows what they look like, not even me, the narrator. I only know their age because they shared it with their listeners during a previous broadcast.

Slight feedback happens with one of the microphones. A voice with enough exuberance to deaf a child speaks, "what is happening, my fellow anomalies. I'm Roc, and sitting next to me is Harde. Come on, Harde, greet our listeners."

And with an unenthusiastic tone, Harde responds, "hey."

"Wow, that's even worse than yesterday's response."

"Yep."

With a clear of his throat, Roc says, "you are tuned in to one three three Roc Harde A.M., the only government-free radio station in the greater New York area. As well as the only station that plays the hardest rock and the nastiest metal. Before we get into our first song, Wake Up by Suicide Silence, it's time for another installment of Indiscretions from the Incognito."

The rapid-fire sound of an air horn plays on the radio, followed by the high-pitched moan of a barely legal teenage girl. They started almost every broadcast with this segment; I haven't missed any of their tales.

The high-pitched moan fades out, and Roc begins to speak again, "Whew! That was loud. I'm glad the neighbors don't have a baby."

Harde responds, "the neighbors are gay."

"That they are."

"Yep."

With an even quicker rebuttal, Roc replies, "It's called adoption, Harde. It's not like we're in the eighties. Speaking of the eighties, the tale we will be telling you today is from the eighties."

With an effortless transition, Harde spoke, "brunettes with big ole bushes giving blowjobs."

"That's right, Harde! Today's tale is titled *The Bashful British Brunette's Beautiful Blowjob*."

"It's a real tear-jerker."

"That was a good one, Harde."

And for the first time this whole morning, Harde, with an ounce of enthusiasm in his voice, replied, "thank you! Thank you."

Now with an imposing tone in his voice, Roc began to speak. "Our story starts with a British woman named Sally Stevens. She quickly walked through the front gates of a coed public school called Morning Glory High, wearing a black pantsuit and flat dress shoes. Her brunette hair looked as soft as soft-serve and curled up to a fine point at her shoulders.

"The next scene was her entering a classroom, and this is where it started to get good, isn't that right, Harde?"

"Yep, the actors' true talents shine here."

Roc continues to speak. "Sally entered the classroom, and all of the students' eyes laser-focused on her. Her double-d breasts would have almost all but protruded out of her white undershirt if not for the thin row of buttons running vertically along its center. Walking in front of the chalkboard, she wrote her name and spoke, 'good morning, class. My name is Dr. Sally Stevens. I'll be your homeroom teacher for the year.' The camera panned out as she wrote on the board and spoke to the class behind her. This is when we see one of her love interests.

"Most of the males in the classroom chatted among themselves, commenting on how robust Sally's ass was and how badly they wanted to get up in there. The camera then focused on a lanky tall white British teen with slicked-back hair and a dangling inverted cross earring on his left ear. He was just sitting there (legs up on the desk with his black and white chucks, sleeveless tank top, and ripped black Levi jeans) doodling anarchy symbols in a marble notebook.

"Her face was bright red as she heard what the male students were saying about her ass, and she left as quickly as she came in. And do you want to tell our listeners what happened next, Harde?"

"I guess." And with all the energy he can muster, which isn't much, Harde continues the tale. "The tall white

British teen walked out shortly after, and then the scene changes once again."

"That's right, Harde. He gallantly chases her down the hallway and sees her dash into the teachers' bathroom. He then catches the door with his foot and follows her in, locking it right after."

Harde interjects. "For privacy, of course."

"Sally turns around after hearing the door lock. Instead of freaking out as most women would, the scene cuts again, and the nameless boy and Sally sit side by side against the white tiled bathroom wall."

Harde interjects again, "a major plot hole appears here."

"Yes, Harde, they don't tell the watcher why they suddenly feel so comfortable with each other, but nobody watches niche eighties blowjob porn for the story."

"I do, Roc. What's the point of all this setup if they don't plan on explaining stuff? Why don't they just start at the fellatio scene if the story isn't important?"

"I don't know, Harde, ask the creators. Oh wait, you can't because this isn't a legal radio program."

"Piss off!"

"There you go, Harde, finally some enthusiasm in your voice. To finish off our tale, Sally unbuttons the lanky British boy's jeans and gives him the most beautiful blowjob I have ever seen. The light gurgling sound due to just the right amount of saliva. Such perfection! Like it was drafted up by a greek mathematician. The camera slowly panned out during this scene, it showed us just enough to know what's happening but not too much to ruin the artistry, and then the end screen appeared. I could go on forever with how perfect the last scene is, but we just ran out of time."

"Yes, we did, Roc."

"That's right, Harde, by now, your wives are most likely done putting on their hour's worth of makeup, so we will now switch over to regularly scheduled programming. It is now six o'clock and sunny in the Country Club area. We welcome you again to Roc Harde A.M. Radio. This is Wake Up by Suicide Silence; enjoy!"

"Enjoy."

Music starts to play simultaneously from digital clocks in houses located all around the surrounding area. The husbands' wives walk out of their bathrooms like clockwork and the day officially starts.

Chapter Three: The Bashful British Brunette

Our age gap

(you're eighteen

& I'm thirty-five)

is a cliche taboo.

Despite my appearance,

I'm really quite shy.

I'm a good catholic woman.

Except for that one time,

that one time in high school

I seductively ate a banana

while sitting at the back pew of a church.

That day,

my presence was a goldmine.

The priest,

my father;

was shocked by the line.

And ever since that day,

I knew my mouth was divine.

Chapter Four: The Gathering of the Neo-Wasps

The atmosphere is depressing again today in suburbia.

Twenty-first-century wasps of varying ethnicities simultaneously left their houses with a full face of clown makeup, with the privilege of being rich radiating from their bodies. This happens every morning in the Country Club area. They take their teenage kids to school and parade through the front gates of an illustrious private school I have deemed the St. Francis School of Fraudulent Faith.

A group of students wearing gas masks inaudibly protest about something at the front gate.

A dozen wasps are sitting around a brown round conference table in their flower sundresses and bright pink hairbands.

The first one to speak was the wife of an oil tycoon. The local youth call her leaky Linda. I heard it started one day when she was breastfeeding her youngest near the front gate. After she was done, she walked into the school, and a trail of excess breast milk followed behind her. Roc and Harde talked about it once on their Woman of the Wasp segment: where they dish the dirt on these not so desperate housewives.

Linda—all one hundred and twenty pounds of freckled whiteness—stood up and slammed the table in front of her. Her c-cup breasts, void of the comfort of an undergarment, jiggle slightly under her yellow daffodil sundress. "We need to do something about this blasphemous radio station I heard my husband listening to this morning."

The rest of the women seemed puzzled by what she said. They all hear the music on their husbands' digital clock radios. However, they don't mind it because they're all happy with their domestic lifestyles, and they don't want to mess it up.

In a red rose sundress, an African American woman nicknamed Ticklish Tanya stood up in anger. After some youth saw her getting tickled by her husband through a gap in their living room curtains, she got the nickname.

Tanya shrieks with fury in her voice, "you're worried about some little radio station run by teenagers. You should be worried that half the student body is boycotting at the front gate because the principal suspended a male student for passing gas during mass."

And with a touch of British comfort, Linda responds with, "I assure you we will figure out how to handle that. However, these two teenagers talked about how they followed one of their female teachers into the staff-only bathroom, locked the door behind them, and then received fellatio from her. They said she was a bashful British woman with a big bush named Sally. Now I, for one, will not tolerate sex between students and teachers or any sex before marriage for that matter, so what are we going to do about it?"

With a laugh aimed at Linda, Tanya said, "you're crazy, you know that. The only thing British we have in this school are the teabags in the cupboard behind me. Your husband was probably just watching porn on his phone again while you were getting ready."

Much like Sally, Linda flew out of the room—leaky breasts and all—after being called crazy in front of her fellow wasps. She left the school shortly after, walking back past the protestors who were now farting into megaphones, and returned to her husband's million-dollar house with determination in her eyes. With no one in the group believing her, she had to get her hands dirty, and this time it wouldn't be from gardening.

Back at the meeting, Ticklish Tanya continued to talk about the student protest outside. Eventually, the conversation went nowhere; nobody wanted to speak up. They didn't want to risk that they, too, would be attacked with words. It continued like this for another twenty minutes until they all simultaneously got up, not having brought up a single way to stop what was happening at the school gates. They all went home to their overpriced houses and white picket fences. They continued to be the not so desperate housewives their husbands knew and loved.

Chapter Five: Natural Gases

We will not be shushed.

We will not be hushed.

Our bowels are not your property.

Our spirits will not be crushed.

We will not be hushed.

We will not be shushed.

Your actions are not scholarly.

Our bowels will not be cuffed.

BRRT!

BRRRRRT!

BREEEEEEEEEEEE!

Even god farts,

because in this universe,

he is but a flea.

Chapter Six: The False Report

A half-moon hangs loose in the sky.

Leaky Linda could now be seen talking with a heavyset Italian man sitting at the front desk of the newly formed, practically fictional, Country Club police precinct. When you have money: power, you can restructure society any way you wish.

With power reinforcing her vocal cords (still wearing her yellow daffodil sundress), she screeches, "officer Stromboli, I have a crime to report."

And with breasts bigger than Linda's, the police officer leans over and snarkily says, "oh really now. Miss Lombardi, did somebody spray paint another pair of lactating breasts on your garage door?"

Tantruming almost like a toddler, Linda replies, "no, they did not. Do you want to arrest some criminals or not?"

"Yeah, okay, I'm listening."

"Two local teenagers who run an illegal radio station called Roc Harde A.M. were bragging about how they snuck into St. Francis and raped one of the teachers."

With a disinterested look on his face, officer Stromboli asks, "and do you know the name of this teacher?"

"Sally, they said her name was Sally: a British woman with brunette hair."

"And did they say how it happened?"

"They followed her into the staff-only bathroom and held her against the bathroom wall."

"Did they lock the door?"

"Yes, and they videotaped themselves taking turns with her."

"Okay, Miss Lombardi, we will get right on it."

"You better, or I will. We don't need these sorts of things happening in our community."

Leaky Linda walks out of the police station, and officer Strumboli leans back in his chair. He didn't write down a single word Linda said to him; he just laughed it off.

A fellow officer—short and buff and whiter than a piece of linen—walks up to officer Stromboli and asks him what Leaky Linda wanted.

Stromboli sits upright to properly face him and says, "This broad is crazy, Jeremy."

"Oh yeah, did someone draw another pair of leaky breasts on her garage door?"

"No, nothing like that. She tried to report the porn Roc and Harde were talking about."

"I guess mister oil tycoon had the radio volume up to high."

"She thought they snuck into St. Francis and raped a British teacher."

"Does St. Francis of the Fraudulent Faith have any British teachers?"

"I wish it did; British women are hot. I heard they still let it grow out down there."

These two officers of the law—who, without a doubt, partake in the illegal listening of Roc Harde A.M.—continue to chat back and forth about how crazy Leaky Linda is.

The night is now over, and husbands from all around suburbia set their alarm clocks for five o'clock. All the wasps lie down in their beds with designer face masks on and go to sleep next to their wealthy husbands, full of privilege; entitlement.

Chapter Seven: A Wasp With a Weapon

Don't come any closer.

If you do, I swear to god

I will shoot your dysfunctioned dick off.

Listening to this smut every morning,

I can't take it anymore.

Urinating into the mouth of a maid.

The rape of a school teacher.

How could you,

my fracker,

make light of these sins,

even after what happened to me.

Twenty years of marriage

fractured by a gang of men.

You smirked at the thought of a dirty me:

of a broken soul;

of a bruised knee.

BANG!

Your reaction is what ruined me.

Chapter Eight: A Cry for Help in a Laundromat?

On an ordinary Wednesday, and I know it was a Wednesday because I didn't have class that day, I woke up around ten o'clock. I gulped down an extra-tall cup of coffee; it had enough almond milk to turn it white and enough sugar to kill a diabetic. This was just the way I liked it.

As I finished gulping it down, I heard keys dancing on the other side of the apartment door. Instantly I knew who it was. The only other person who could have been home at this time was my father. And as I had thought that, a short Italian man with no hair and a gut the size of a half-term pregnant woman came walking through the door. His hands were tripled up with Key Food bags, and in his mouth, a device the size of a USB stick was lighting up green.

He placed the bags down on the kitchen floor. He then took the USB-looking device out of his mouth, which let out a cloud of cotton candy smog, and said to me, "the clothes are drying at the laundromat; get dressed and go get them."

My voice was coated with reluctance as someone who had just woken up, and I said, "fine, just let me put some clothes on and go to the bathroom before you rush me outside."

Despite having that extra tall cup of coffee, I didn't speed up. I grabbed my Monster Energy hoodie and my beaten-up vans at an amputees pace, put them on, and headed out the door.

What was actually a block and a half walk felt like a death march. After about two minutes I arrived. I walked past the infamous patch of dead grass with the sign that said chemicals keep off the grass and made my way up a hill that is just a random set of storefronts. First, there was a barbershop, then a fitness studio with a weight watchers office attached to it. And then, after a driveway, there are three more stores, a pizza shop, the laundromat, and a nail salon.

I made my way into the laundromat and was met with the usual glare from the Asian American owners standing at the folding tables in front of me. The dryers were all lined up and numbered at the back of the place. One through thirteen, each one was stickered a corresponding number in reverse from right to left.

On my way over to dryer number six, I noticed a quarter-aged white woman and an adolescent white girl standing at the opposite end of the folding tables from where the owners were. The woman, at first glance, seemed normal, but the girl seemed off; the air around her was chaotic. She couldn't stop moving. She was vigorously pulling the woman's arm as she moved back and forth, almost like she was trying to rip it off.

I continued onward to my dryer and when I got there, there was a black garbage bag hanging from the handle. My dad had left it there; he always did.

As I was throwing the dry clothes into the garbage bag, I could hear the girl speak. At first, it was like she was speaking an alien language, but that might have just been my lack of sense perception. I have spent many hours blasting heavy metal music through my speakers.

When I finally heard what she was saying, I almost lost it. It took what little energy I had (the coffee still hadn't kicked in yet) to not laugh out loud. She screamed, what sounded like it was through a loudspeaker, "I'm going to stick a fork in an outlet. I'm going to stick a fork in an outlet." And at that moment, I knew it wasn't something to laugh at, but it was so unexpected that I couldn't help but laugh internally.

The girl obviously had some mental disability, so she didn't know any better. However, the woman who looked perfectly sane at the time also looked like she didn't know any better. So when the look on this woman's face was as if she had already said something once before, I couldn't help but think that this was an everyday event. But even if this did happen every day, it was as if all the woman thought she had to do was tell the girl to stop, and she would stop. It's as if something in her brain told her that words alone were enough to calm this twister of a child.

This woman, before my eyes, was sinking into herself, and I got a drive-by view of it. That discomfort you get when you have to piss in public is exactly how she looked. Her knees were tucked inward, she was in some sort of half-crouch, and her face reeked of embarrassment.

And then I walked past them and went outside.

Walking by, internally laughing with a smile on my face, further affected the atmosphere of the laundromat.

When I turned around to sneak another look, I saw them exit.

I carried the dry clothes home and didn't really think much of it at the time. Still, as I'm recalling it now, it makes me believe that this whole encounter was a delusion caused by an excessive intake of caffeine. Did I really witness such an unusual event, or am I the one with a severe mental disability? If I ever see that woman and child again, I will have my answer.

Chapter Nine: Just a Dead Patch of Grass

Am I just a dead patch of grass?

A rusty collection of blades

that gets pissed on by persons best friend.

A burden of the lower class.

If I am that dead patch of grass,

why was I drowned with chemicals

and left to decay.

Was my caretaker blind that day?

No longer capable of flapping in the wind.

No longer able to feel the dew.

Empty and lifeless.

Just another day of feeling blue.

Chapter Ten: How to Kidnap Someone in Broad Daylight;

Player One: Kassandra the Kidnapped

Kassandra awakens from her slumber every morning like a Greek goddess after an orgy. On this particular day, she woke up in her king-sized bed surrounded by naked men and women of various shapes and sizes. As an American—with Greek roots on her mothers side going back to Delphi—she embodies a powerful creative, like those from Joe Hill's NOS4A2. The only difference is that it doesn't get her killed. She bends the material world to her will through art, sex, art sex, and sex art and her bubbly demeanor allows for even the most prudish of people to put aside their practices for a session of pleasure.

Walking out of her million-dollar house in yesterday's clothing: black Louis Vuitton flats, Lord and Taylor belted floral pants, and a black v-neck tie-hem blouse, she gets into her 2020 Toyota Prius Prime. Once a week, she drives to the bank to replenish her spending money. Her brother left her a large sum.

Inside the bank, next in line for the only teller available, she says, "what a lovely day it is today."

A Puerto Rican woman with various eczema blotches running up and down her neck speaks from behind the row of teller windows in a tired voice, despite being only half-past nine, "next."

Kassandra walks up to the middle teller window. She reads the nametag on the eczema-ridden woman's Chase employee t-shirt and greets her. "Good morning!

Emilia! My name's Kassandra! You have such a lovely name!"

And without an ounce of reaction, Emilia responds, "what will it be?"

Before Kassandra could answer, a group of individuals wearing nineties cartoon character masks stormed into the bank.

One of them, wearing a Chuckie mask from Rugrats, shoots his Glock 19 at the ceiling of the bank and yells out, "everybody on the ground. If anybody moves, they will start a very intimate relationship with one of my bullets."

With everybody face-first on the ground, an individual wearing a Johnny Bravo mask walks up to where Kassandra is, grabs her, and carries her over his shoulder to the bank entrance.

The rest of the intruders—one wearing a Courage the Cowardly Dog mask, the one in the Chuckie mask, and a couple wearing Ren and Stimpy masks—all ran out the door.

Kassandra trys to greet her kidnapper. "Hey! How's it going! What's your name!"

The person carrying Kassandra doesn't respond; he just follows the rest out of the bank.

All Kassandra could think of, at this moment, was this person's muscles were beautiful. I wonder if he would be willing to do some modeling. Even during this supposed traumatic event, Kassandra remained friendly and easygoing despite knowing the possibilities of what could happen to her.

Chapter Eleven: The Trust in Trust Fund

Brother,

I love you,

but you broke the trust in trust fund.

You gave me all this money,

but you never told me how you obtained it.

One day,

you disappeared,

and all you said to me was,

don't trust anybody;

all our neighbors are animals.

What could I have done with that knowledge?

I would have just preferred the truth.

The truth is more important to me

than any amount of money.

Brother,

you left me alone,

and now the animals

try to waltz through my home.

If you were still around,

I wouldn't be edging towards the catacomb.

Chapter Twelve: HTKSIBD; Player Two:

Emilia, the Eczematic Exenthusiast

Emilia wakes up every morning in her two-bedroom apartment like a slug with a hangover. She heads to the bathroom right after waking up and applies an ample amount of hydrocortisone to the blotches of rough skin living on various parts of her body.

She's alone again this morning. Her son stays at her ex-husband's house after a messy breakup; her Puerto Rican spice died. What a terrible thing to say to your spouse.

Emilia gets ready for work and drags it out for as long as possible, exhaling the words, "I'm going to quit," repeatedly under her breath.

It has been two hours, and Emilia now sits in a chair behind a sheet of bullet-resistant plexiglass. Emilia stares off towards the entrance of the Chase bank where she works and spots an overly bubbly brunette woman walking through the door. The woman gets in line to use the teller and says out loud, with enough force to break the plexiglass, what a lovely day it is today.

Emilia hears her and, under her breath, says, "oh great, one of these people." Finishing up with her current customer, she says "next," and the bubbly brunette walks up to her.

With an abundance of excitement, the bubbly brunette says, "morning! Emilia! My name's Kassandra! You have such a lovely name!"

And without an ounce of reaction, Emilia responds with, "what will it be?"

Before Kassandra could respond, a group of individuals wearing the faces of nineties cartoon characters burst into the bank. Emilia chuckled; it was her first one in weeks.

One of them was wearing a Chuckie mask from Rugrats; he shot his Glock 19 at the bank's ceiling and yelled, "everybody down on the ground. If anybody moves, they will start a very intimate relationship with one of my bullets."

Under her breath, Emilia continued to chuckle. She knew the severity of the situation but couldn't help but think that it would be her first intimate relationship with something in months if she took a bullet.

Everybody in the bank was now face down on the ground except for Emilia; she was standing stiff with a smirk on her face. The place she hated to work at was getting robbed in front of her own eyes.

An individual wearing a Johnny Bravo mask walks up to where Emilia and Kassandra are, lifts Kassandra up from the floor, carries her over his shoulder, and walks off.

The remainder of the masked individuals, the one wearing the Chuckie mask, one wearing a Courage the Cowardly Dog Mask, and a couple wearing Ren and Stimpy masks, follow Johnny Bravo out the door.

Emilia, through the plexiglass, hears Kassandra trying to engage in conversation. She is dumbfounded that a group of individuals with masks run into a bank to kidnap a woman. She repeatedly says, just loud enough for others to hear, "what the fuck just happened?"

The cops showed up shortly after. Emilia answered all their questions, returning to work after: returning to her normal melancholic state. She never forgot what happened; she wished for something else to excite her.

Chapter Thirteen: You Could Kidnap Me Any Day

Oh,

Johnny,

you are so dreamy.

At least, I think you are.

When I replay the incident in my head

your charm is hidden.

You could kidnap me any day.

Chapter Fourteen: HTKSIBD; Player Three:

Kane of the Kid Kidnapers

Every morning, Kane rolls out of bed like the leftover grease from an obese man's fourth plate of Walmart bacon. Squished around him—because they all share a king-sized bed—are his four other foster siblings, Charlie, Emanuel, Tyriel, and Ruth. Charlie, the oldest, is always the last one to get out of bed. Kane is always the first one up; the demons of his dreams refuse to let him sleep anymore.

By the time everyone else gets up, Kane has already gone through multiple hours of television programming: watching old cartoons on Boomerang. His foster parents often work double shifts at Jacobi Hospital as Emergency Room doctors, which allows him to watch television at odd hours without any objection.

One morning, after all of his foster siblings woke up, he told them of the brilliant idea he had while watching television the night before. They were all eager to hear his plan. His previous ones had made them a little extra spending money, so they were ready for anything. He told them he had purchased nineties cartoon character masks off the internet. That they would kidnap a rich woman in a bank and hold her hostage in her own million-dollar mansion. How every day before school started, he crossed paths with this woman that reeked of riches and sunshine and that he had followed her back to where she lived. He told them they would be the wealthiest foster teenagers in the Pelham Bay area if they did everything he instructed.

It is now the day of the kidnapping. Kane and his foster siblings are standing outside the bank. They carefully watch and wait for the rich women to walk up to the only available teller.

The woman walks up to the teller.

They all begin to put their masks on and untuck the Glocks from their pants—Charlie with his Chuckie mask, Emanual with his Courage the Cowardly Dog mask, Tyriel with his Ren mask, and Ruth with her Stimpy mask.

Kane says with confidence, muffled through his Johnny Bravo mask, "Chuckie, you go in first and shoot a couple Glock rounds into the ceiling. Threaten to shoot them if they do anything funny. Then I'll run in and make my way over to the target. Courage, you watch the entrance. Ren and Stimpy, you keep an eye on the other customers."

Chuckie shakes his head and runs into the bank, shooting up into the ceiling and yelling the words, "everybody down on the ground. If anybody moves, they will start a very intimate relationship with one of my bullets."

Johnny runs in next. All of the patrons are now face-first on the ground. He walks over to the target, a brunette woman wearing Lord and Taylor clothes and Louis Vuitton flats.

Courage, Ren, and Stimpy enter shortly after Johnny. Ren and Stimpy wave their guns around at the patrons on the floor, and Courage stands near the entrance.

Johnny picks the woman up off the ground, tosses her over his shoulder, and says under his breath, "for a woman in her mid-twenties, she sure is light. I wonder if she has an eating disorder like Ruth."

The woman on Johnny's shoulders speaks enthusiastically as she is carried out, "hey! How's it going! What's your name!"

Johnny, at this point, is wondering how the person he kidnapped could possibly be so friendly at a time like this. Ignoring her, he runs out the door, with his siblings following after him. He then throws her into the trunk of a double-parked used green 2004 Chevrolet Impala, and they

take off.

Chapter Fifteen: Cartoons on the Brain

If life was a cartoon,

we could stay

the same age forever.

We would be in the same grade

for twenty years

while our creators get paid.

We could wander the suburb never afraid.

If life was a cartoon,

then we would be the villains;

the delinquents that skip class

and spraypaint over signs

that say, keep off the grass.

If life was a cartoon,

our every action

would be determined for us.

If I was a cartoon character,

I would want to kill myself.

Getting used by future generations is akin to death.

Chapter Sixteen: Is it Kosher to Kiss Your Kidnappers?

Getting kidnapped is one of the scariest things that can happen to either you or a loved one. However, for a select few, their reaction is outrageous. Some kidnap their kidnappers while others kiss them.

Statues of various geometric shapes appear to be scattered around the front yard of Kassandra's house. If you draw a line connecting them, the ultimate shape gets made: two outward-facing trapezoids with a horizontal colon in the center. It is worshipped by non-magical conspiracy theorists; they believe it can lead to the unknown.

The house itself was one of those super modern cube ones.

Kane and his siblings roll up to the house after following a circle driveway (slowly as not to alert the neighbors). His face, as well as his siblings, were no longer covered.

One at a time, they exit the Green Chevrolet Impala. It must have been stolen because their foster parents always took the bus to work.

Ruth, Tyriel, and Emanuel exited the backseat first. They are triplets with curly brown hair, hazelnut skin, and a height only an inch taller than a mailbox.

Charlie got out of the passenger seat next. He was five feet five inches, had ivory skin, and a buzz cut of burnt orange hair.

Lastly, Kane left the driver's seat. His bald head, chalk skin, and six-foot stature became exposed to the outside world. Despite going outside every day, his skin never tanned.

Everybody was wearing the same outfit: blue dungarees, a white Hanes t-shirt, and a pair of white Vans that were practically black.

Walking over to the Impala's trunk Kane waited for it to pop open; he had hit the latch before leaving the car.

Kassandra confidently peeked out of the trunk with a smile on her face.

"Hey there, Bubbles," Kane said jokingly. "Unless you want to be another lawn ornament, do as I say."

No response.

Dragging Kassandra out of the trunk, Kane lifts her over his shoulder. He then carries her over to the front porch and enters the house.

An open-door policy is practiced in this household. Everybody else follows after him.

The inside of Kassandra's house was just as unique as she was. Every inch of the interior was filled with the same symbol that made up the front lawn.

"Wow, lady," Ruth spoke for the first time in a soft tone while looking around the house, "you're awful at interior decorating."

"Ruth, no talking," Charlie ordered with a deep, authoritative tone as he and the rest of his siblings walked into the kitchen.

Slamming Kassandra down on the white marble kitchen counter, even this had symbols, Kane walks over to the sink. The back of her head was now bleeding.

Grabbing a dirty scotch glass from the sink, Kane walks back to Kassandra and puts its underside on her lips. With his left hand, he pulls a hidden Smith and Wesson 10mm revolver out from the front of his dungarees, placing the barrel inside the glass. "Where do you keep your valuables?"

Kassandra couldn't speak with a glass covering her mouth; she didn't need to. Puckering her lips, she kissed the scotch glass, and it melted. A green-like secretion of liquid was now coated on her lips.

"The fuck," Kane said while jumping backward, trying to distance himself from Kassandra so that he could figure out his next move.

Now able to talk, Kassandra regains her bubbly demeanor. She hops down off the kitchen counter and says, "relax." There was a small amount of blood on the counter where her head was; no indication of a wound was on the back of her head. "Have a nice rest," Kassandra added while blowing the green-like liquid into the faces of her kidnappers.

One at a time, Kane and his siblings ragdolled onto the floor.

A knock at the front door breaks the confusion in the air.

"Ms. Geary," a short and buff Italian man with a brown buzzcut called out as he knocked on the door. "It's Officer Alesi. You know, Jeremy, we went to school together."

The front door opened very slightly, and Kassandra peeked her head out. "hello. How can I help you this time?"

"Nosy Nataly is at it again." Officer Alesi replied without an ounce of professionalism.

"The car."

"Yeah, and your kidnapping."

"Oh, that. It's taken care of." Kassandra opens the door. She pulls a stack of twenty 100 dollar bills out of her pant pocket. She then slides it into the front pocket of officer Alesi's uniform. "Dump the car for me, near the cove of turtles."

"You got it, ma'am."

Kassandra closes the door.

Officer Alesi gets in the car and takes off. His state of the art police issue bicycle is left abandoned on the driveway. Let's hope nobody steals it.

Back inside the house, in the living room, to be exact, a bright light is escaping outward towards the front door. A pair of black steel doors manifest directly on top of an ultimate symbol at the center of the floor.

Running over to where the light is (Kassandra has only seen this phenomenon once before, but she knows exactly what it is), she screams, "Gerard!"

Popping head first out of the portal were Gerard and Karrine. They were wearing the same outfits as before. For Karrine, it was an atomic blonde neck-length wig, black chinos, a purple spaghetti strap top, and black two-inch heels. And for Gerard: knee ripped skinny jeans, a sleeveless black tee, and a pair of double comfort Crocs.

After leaving Pangea, Gerard dropped off almost all the deserters at the Grey Eel Estate. He then returned to his birthplace for the first time in years. He wasn't homesick; he knew that his sister would be okay with housing a dimensional alien.

"Quiet down, will ya," Gerard said tiringly as he looked around the house. "I'm glad you kept the wallpaper."

"Bro, I missed you." Kassandra ran up to him and gave him a hug. She then backs up and smacks him across the face.

Karrine cuts in on the family reunion. "I like her," she said seductively.

"The fuck, Kaz." Gerard expressed without even flinching.

Kassandra didn't respond to her brother's provocation. However, she darts out of the living room and returns to the kitchen, where Kane and his siblings are still unconscious.

Having followed Kassandra into the kitchen, Karrine sees five kids passed out on the floor. "Da fuk," she articulated poorly with a change of accent so significant it was like she was born in The Bronx. "I knew this was too good to be true."

"Calm down," said Gerard nonchalantly as he walked over to his sister's kidnappers. Everyone was piled on the floor between the island and the stove. Grabbing Ruth's right leg, Gerard pulls her from the pile and asks, "Kaz, are they alive?"

"Yeah," Kassandra replied, the smile still on her face. "I've been studying the tome you gave me for Christmas."

"That's good." Gerard drags Ruth into the hallway, placing her on a symbol on the floor. He repeats this four times and says to Karrine, "come here. You need to see this."

Reluctantly, Karrine stands behind Gerard and peaks over his shoulder.

Stomping once on the floor, a tingle shoots up Gerard's leg.

All five symbols glow a bright white, morphing into black steel doors. The weight of the bodies pushes open the doors, and they simultaneously fall, disappearing into alien planets.

"Well, what was that supposed to show me?" Karrine asked in a confused manner.

"Never underestimate anybody on this planet—" Gerard started to say.

"—because if you do," Kassandra interjected. "You'll get thrown into the unknown."

Karrine didn't know how to respond anymore to the discussion at hand. She had finally received her wish: to live in a world where her transformation isn't perceived as a magician's curse. Doing anything else except settling down would be a detriment to her life.

Chapter Seventeen: Interplanetary Alien

A change of location

doesn't erase your reputation.

The eyes of the judgers

follow you through even the abyss,

leeching onto the disapproval

of like-minded otherworlders.

I'm just an interplanetary alien.

Even with an artificial body

I can't escape the haters.

It's like I'm their hobby.

Free and honest.

Honest with myself

about who I am.

No book or chromosome

can tell me otherwise.

I'm an alien,

and I'm okay with it.

Chapter Eighteen: The Kunoichi

The year is 1603, in the Edo period of feudal Japan. This is what she tells people when they see her. She roams around in the night, for she and the darkness are in cahoots. Her jet black hair is tied back and held in place with a tortoiseshell comb that's painted gold. A fox mask covers her face, and fishnet stockings lay upon her praying mantis legs.

On top of that lies a pair of cherry blossom hotpants that she made herself. An open see-through black mesh long sleeve shirt rests upon her shoulders, exposing her midsection. Her breasts are wrapped tightly with gauze squeezing them together like a Victorian woman in a corset. Completely covering the front side of her neck is a tattoo of a female black swallowtail butterfly. And lastly, running down the front side of her left arm to her hand is a tattoo of connecting pink lotus flowers.

For her, these are the markings of her clan; it's all she has to remember them by. On that fateful night in the year 1591, during her twelfth birthday, her family was attacked. Since then, she has carried the burden of exacting revenge on the people who did it. With the help of her super-secret cultivation techniques, she sees the surrounding world through heartbeats and auras, attacking and subduing the people who wronged her family. Her will in this fight is as strong as the pressure from the waterfall she trained under, and nothing will stop her, not the Tokugawa shogunate or the people in white.

The year is actually 2022, and the Kunoichi is a woman by the name of Sandra Smith. As a child, she used this exuberant: dark tale in an attempt to bond with her father in a household filled with mostly boys. Her biological mother had given her up after birth. She was placed in the foster care system until the age of twelve. When she finally got adopted, it was by a wealthy celebrity couple who had an addiction to adopting kids for social glory, like Madonna but less successful.

As the only daughter this couple had, she was poked and prodded by the paparazzi everywhere she went. Eventually, she turned to drugs, and it was during this time the world believed that she had lost her way. She went out partying every night, snorting cocaine off of strangers' asses in bathroom stalls, even getting the butterfly and lotus tattoos that she had made up as a child.

At the age of eighteen, she overdosed, and the story of the vengeful kunoichi came to life. Her worlds crashed together like two roman candles pointed at each other, and ever since then, she has lived within the delusion. She ran around in her ninja outfit and attacked people she believed hurt her clan. The news called her the paparazzi killer, leaving behind a pink lotus flower in the mouths of her targets.

She now sits on death row with weekly visits from her adoptive parents, who thank her for the publicity. She also gets visits from a Christian pastor, who she believes is trying to disrupt her cultivation in the ways of Ninpo. In her cell, she often meditates only to be interrupted, with her enhanced senses, by the noisy life outside.

Chapter Nineteen: A Butterfly with Weighted Wings.

Oh!

The chaos it brings.

Chapter Twenty: Our Lady of Perpetual Silence

Eighteen years ago.

A straw basket is found on the cement chapel steps of St. Francis of the Fraudulent Faith. All the nuns maternally flock around the basket to see what was inside it, and only seconds later, they let out a chorus of screams. What they saw was an abomination. It had pale skin black hair, and its mouth was professionally sewn shut. Just beside it was a note that said do with her as you please, for she is a soldier of Satan.

Despite all the signs present in front of the nuns, their faith made it impossible to abandon the child. With this moral practice in hand, the nuns took the basket off the steps and went into the church. The inside was filled with malicious air; it emanated from the basket.

A pastor was standing over an altar at the other end of the building. With a loud voice, he told the nuns to "place the basket on the altar and leave at once."

The first thing the preacher did was pull out the thread holding her mouth shut. Not a single sound came out afterward. He began to examine her body to see if anything else was wrong with her. A shadow formed as the preacher held her body up to the sunlight seeping through the ceiling cracks. The shadow stood on the wall. Instead of the shadow of a normal baby, it was the shadow of a screaming baby. On this day, the preacher vowed to raise the girl as his own; he named her Abigail.

For the next seventeen years, Abigail lived a relatively healthy life. She went to school and did her duties for the preacher. There was only one problem with her, she never talked. The trauma of having her mouth sewn shut as a baby left some lingering demons. On top of living in the church attic, she never got a straight answer from the nuns about who her parents were. They would always avoid her and look at her like she had horns growing out of her head.

On the day of her eighteenth birthday, she came home from school to find the church was empty. Not a soul in sight. She could feel something was off, almost like her being a mute gave her other senses a boost. She knew she was alone, but she could hear an organ playing "Lacrimosa" by Wolfgang Amadeus. She heard it all the time when she participated in the funeral gatherings. The weeping civilians would always fill the air with sadness and despair; it became relaxing to Abigail. Though, this time was different.

While walking up the aisle, she peeked left and right into the rows of pews. One after another, the bodies of her fellow churchgoers came into view, mutilated and scorched with pieces scattered in every direction.

Abigail moved forward despite her now shaky legs. When she finally got to the altar, she was met with a chill colder than Antarctica.

What she saw next would have left anybody screaming in terror, but for Abigail, there was nothing. The sight of the one that raised her with his chest pried open like he was in the middle of heart surgery. Blood leaking out of the perfectly placed cuts up and down his body.

Abigail stood there, not because of shock but due to a lack of sympathy. She knew something was wrong with her. While standing there, an outline forms on the floor beneath her feet.

After a couple of seconds, the design comes into shape. Two outward-facing trapezoids fused together with a horizontal colon can now be seen on the floor beneath Abigail. She is now puzzled by the symbol.

The Order of Perpetual Silence is a sub-congregation of Catholicism that studies from the Tome of Silent Shapes. They act like ordinary Catholics in front of others, but their practices actually create results. All of their original practices were created by a single man. The man who took in Abigail, Augustus Geary. He found a way to use shapes and the silent sounds they make to trap evil. This made the evil in the world wary of his very existence; they would never dare step foot in his church. It wasn't until his son started practicing that it turned into a way to hop dimensions.

Each half of the colon acts like a doorknob. However, you don't actually need to turn it. When the blood of the trapper drips onto the door, it opens.

The blood leaking out of Augustus was puddling up around Abigail's bare feet. The door opens inward, and without even flinching, Abigail begins to fall. Falling to what felt like her death should have given her the right to scream her lungs out, but this still wasn't the case. During her fall, she wasn't alone; a shadow could be seen jumping through the door after her.

Abigail came to an abrupt stop after falling about two meters. Hitting the ground feet first, she shattered them completely. Not a word was said, but tears started pouring out of her eyes. Lying on the floor, she stayed there, helpless with no way to escape. After some time, she fell asleep on the brimstone floor.

Even in her dreams, she didn't speak.

When Abigail woke up, a creature with a swan's head and a human's body was sitting near her. It was watching her. Still groggy from the pain she felt during the shattering of her bones, she tilts her head up to the best of her ability and faces the creature.

The creature starts to speak. "Oh, my precious child, you have suffered immensely from the greed of others. To have been abandoned by your foster parents at such a young age. All because of your peculiar appearance: they were terrified of you. Not knowing how to handle you, they abandoned you on chapel steps and blamed it on a difference of religion. They called you a devil and silenced you the only way they knew how but it's over now; you don't have to worry anymore. I will ease your pain."

Abigail's legs were as good as new with a snap of the creature's fingers. Even with the miracle of healed bones, not a word was uttered.

Instead of getting angry at her continued silence, he introduced himself to her. "My name is Cygnus Atratus, and I am a beacon of death. I appear where misfortune happens, and then I tell this planet's reaper where the bodies are. Though, this time was different; I was here for personal business. I came to get my daughter back, and the pastor got in my way, so I removed him and the nuns from my path.

"I will now tell you about the day of your conception. One night on my way back to the River of Styx, I laid my eyes upon a beautiful white swan. Her name was Cygnus Olor, and she is known as the beacon of life. Everywhere she went, life was made. On that day, our gazes crossed, and our forbidden love bloomed.

"I know this might be hard to believe, but I am your father. Your dark black hair is what you took from me, and your pale white skin was from your mother. After your birth, we had to hide you in the human world. What we didn't think would happen was that the family we left you with would abandon you; they have been punished accordingly. You will now have to make a choice, rot in this hole or stay by my side."

Abigail seemed to be intrigued by what her father was saying. For the first time in her life, she knew something about her origin. She is no longer just Abigail; she is Abigail Atratus, the daughter of a demon. The reason behind her dreadful demeanor and love of funerals was finally given to her. You could actually see a smile forming on her face. She had forgotten entirely about what happened to the pastor and his nuns.

A decision was made. Abigail's mouth begins to move as she speaks for the first time in eighteen years. She says, only producing four words with her underdeveloped vocal cords, "take me with you."

Cygnus extended his arms outward towards Abigail, and within seconds she did the same. Now hugging each other, he opened his retractable black and red onyx wings and flew to the surface with her in both arms.

Chapter Twenty-One: A Human Body, The Most Complex

Shape

In my mother's womb,

I heard the silent sounds of shapes.

She was standing in a supermarket

when a sucker punch to the stomach

transmitted the sound.

Nails on a chalkboard.

A chainsaw to a wall.

Two drunk men and their brawl.

Even this is inadequate.

The pain my mother felt;

the pain I heard,

a physical representation of hell.

Chapter Twenty-Two: The Squealing Widow

Up until an hour ago, Cindy, my mother, was the perfect domestic housewife in the eyes of the catholic church. Pink button-up t-shirts (that showed not even a hint of cleavage) and beige dungaree dress pants (that hid her super-model thigh gap) filled her wardrobe. She took care of the kids, made dinner, and tidied up around the house. She did the once-a-month passionless sex with a husband who consistently left her dry; I overheard them talking once. She was miserable, but at least to the outside world, there was the impression of safety and normalcy. That is all that really matters for the suburban society we live in.

My father, all three hundred pounds of him, died from brain swelling after falling off the treadmill in our two-car garage. His head went full force into the concrete floor and was left lying there for half an hour while my mother went to pick up my younger sister, Amber, from middle school. When she pulled into the driveway (the left garage door had opened due to a sensor on the floor), she slammed on the brakes of her red Nissan Rogue and just sat there.

My sister jumped out of the car right away and ran over to where our father was—practically lifeless—with tears in her eyes. My mother, who was still sitting stationary behind the driver's wheel, wasn't crying or showing any signs of being distraught; she was smiling.

A minute later, she finally exited the vehicle. And with a dark glow radiating off of her, she walked over to the garage, where my father was still slowly dying.

When she arrived, she reached into the right pocket of her pants, pulled out a pink Samsung Galaxy S10 with a fluttering heart case, gave it to my sister, and told her to call 9-1-1.

Soon after, an ambulance pulled up and took my father to Einstein Hospital in the Bronx, where my mother birthed my sister and me. He died during transit, and the rest was textbook. The extended family was notified, and the funeral happened. The grief parade swept through the neighborhood. And eventually, it almost all but disappeared.

Six months have passed since my father's death, and I, Brandon, who recalled this event, am okay now, or at least I think I am. My mother went from being a person who didn't even notice me standing in the driveway (as she sat in her car smiling) to a brand new person. Or was she reverting back to the person she once was?

I saw her smoking today. She was sitting on the front steps holding a bottle of jack and the pack of Camel cigarettes beside her was nearly empty. The dungarees and the button-up t-shirt were gone; they were on fire in the backyard next to the big oak tree and the azaleas. Nothing caught fire unless you count all the ideas spawning in her brain simultaneously. You know what, I'm not okay.

My mother raided my shirt cache again this morning: a wooden box with hand-carved skulls I keep under the floorboards of my room. She took my favorite shirt. My Fearful God shirt from their Pleasure of Sin album. However, she didn't burn it like my other hardcore shirts. When I found her drinking and smoking on the front steps, she had it on, tied up to the side. The three-headed side portrait of Jesus crying was pushed together and filled with excess cigarette ash. But that wasn't the worst of it; she also had on a pair of daisy dukes that a female companion had left in my room one night. For the first time in my life, my mother showed enough skin to make everybody in her old church group shriek. I went straight to sleep after that image was ingrained in my head.

Another week has passed since my father's death. I was about to head out to the chapel at St. Francis, where all the underground concerts happened, when I was suddenly stopped halfway down the front yard by my mother. She was still wearing the same clothes that scarred my eyes, which I assume were washed, at least I hope they were.

"Wait," she frantically called out in a kind of cry.

With a look of annoyance now running across my face, I turn around and say, "mom, I'm leaving, don't try to stop me."

And with a sort of pout on her face, she replies in a soothing tone, "I don't want to stop you, sweetie. Please let me go with you. My Jack and Camels have run out, and I want to have some quality bonding time with you."

The smell of Jack was now hovering around my nose. I wave my hand in front of my face and reluctantly reply, "alright, mom, you can tag along."

My mom and I made our way to the venue, with my mom slowly staggering behind me in a pair of black Converses that I had never seen before and her peach blond hair in a bun.

When we reached the chapel, a giant poster board sign hung from the front entrance, Filth Pit was written on it. We carefully went down the basement steps. It is known by the local scene that the previous preacher's son started the tradition of once-a-month concerts in the basement.

Pushing through a crowd of like-minded individuals, we stood side by side near the group's center as we waited for the band on stage to finish setting up their equipment. The speakers turned on shortly after.

The lead singer picked up the mic stand and yelled into the microphone, "What is up Country Club. We are Fearful God from Greenwich, Connecticut. This first song goes out to a fan of ours who got expelled from school for farting during mass; it's called Force Fed."

They began to play their first song, and we just stood there as others started to open up a circle near us. People around us (all wearing what looked to be the same pair of ripped acid-washed jeans and various other band tees) started piling towards the circle.

The vocalist began to scream, "one at a time, they line us up and shove shit down our throat. The new age is upon us, and religion is no longer an antidote."

I only took my eyes off my mother for a second—to look around us so that we don't get swallowed up by the human tornado that formed—but that was all it took. As soon as those heavy guitar riffs came in, she was gone. She was in the center of the storm, all one hundred and sixty pounds of her, flailing her limbs in various directions. Her hair was no longer in a bun as it was knocked loose by her erratic movements. She didn't last long in the pit, and some big white guy that looked like he was in his thirties, wearing nothing but a speedo and a goatee, pulled her off to the side. I waded back through the crowd and made my way back to her.

Standing next to each other again, my mother turns her head to me, out of breath and her face bright red, and says, "hey sweety, are you having fun? Everybody here is so nice. I'm so sorry about how I acted towards you when your father was still around."

Before I could say anything, the next song started to play. The whole room got loud again. And again, I was left to stand there, conflicted about how I should feel about what my mom said.

People flooded the circle again, and the vocalist sang, "grouped together by designs on a shirt. We, the drove, were driven to this. Reeeeeeeeeeeeeeeeeeeeeeeeeeeeeeeeeeeee!"

As the singer sang those fated words, everyone in the crowd followed suit. Collectively they let out a reeeeeeeeeeeeeeeeeeeeeeeeeeeeeeeeeeee!

I couldn't compose myself; my mother had just pig squealed at maximum volume into my ears. She then tapped on my shoulder, which in concert terms meant she was heading back into the pit, and off she went.

Standing there, all shell-shocked, I was confused about what to do with my mother. She seemed to be having a lot of fun. However, I didn't want to be here for the first time in quite some time. I felt exactly how I felt at church, at my father's funeral, like a kid who just ran up twelve flights of stairs and left his inhaler at home. My usual go-to place for reflection and acceptance had been—at this moment—taken hostage by my drunk, lapsed catholic mother and her want for self-expression.

With the room now spinning faster than the human windmills in the mosh pit, I sprint through the crowd of people. I go up the basement stairs and crouch downward at the chapel entrance, gripping my knees with my hands.

Crouched at the end of the music's reach, I heard the vocalist scream the words all heroes go to hell and sunk even further into the space between my legs. I felt at odds with the world. Why is my life such a shit show? I asked myself this under my breath.

I stood back up and ran off in the opposite direction of where I lived, leaving my mother behind. After about five minutes, I came to an overpass; it connected Country Club to Pelham Bay. Many others have jumped off of this overpass throughout the years (some even in front of me), and they all ended up where they wanted to go. I wasn't sure if I wanted to try it myself; I just wanted the world to stop speaking.

Now, leaning up against the black chainlink fence of the overpass, I say under my breath, "I'll wait ten minutes. If nobody comes for me, I'll do it. If somebody comes for me, maybe I'll still do it."

The sun set, and I stood there for ten minutes uninterrupted, except for the sound of the world that continued to egg me on. Then the lights went out, and the backup generators blew. Silence fell upon my ears. And with this, the world went black.

Chapter Twenty-Three: The Noise of the World

Everything on a planet

contributes to its noise.

The pollution is horrendous,

like a child with his toys.

On and on

the world spins

and the noise spreads out,

traversing the sky

into children with doubt.

Parents never really know

what's going on.

They're always busy

mowing their fucking lawn.

They nag and nag

about the way we dress,

but they don't even try

to relieve our stress.

No god would ever bless this mess.

Chapter Twenty-Four: Patrice the Polynesian Pigeon

Plucker

Even animals grieve their dead; thousands are taken

from their families prematurely due to slaughterhouses and

mechanical mishaps. However, that's not all. Every

generation, people from all around the globe throw rocks at

stray dogs and stomp on earthworms; it's just something

bored people do.

It is the RAWRing 20s, a time when former

myspace scene kids transition into serial killers. These

misunderstood individuals snap after years of teenage angst

and verbal parental abuse.

Patrice is one of these individuals. At twenty-six

years old, he spends his days working at the local

supermarket. At night, he lures naive scene girls to his

one-bedroom apartment with a promise of seeing his vintage 2000s emo vinyl collection.

Patrice didn't start with murdering these girls; he started with the pigeons he kept in a coop on the roof of his apartment complex. The first one was out of anger. His mom left him a voicemail on his answering machine saying that she could no longer send him money on Venmo because his father had found out. Whenever he would get upset, he would climb up to the roof and tend to his pigeons.

Sheila died that night; she was the prettiest of his pigeons. This was the start of what the local newspaper called The Scene Killer. For every pigeon Patrice plucked, he would kill a scene girl with the same name. So when Shelia died, Patrice went to the closest abandoned building he could find and found a girl named Sheila. She had rainbow-colored hair and snakebites; she looked more like a peacock than a pigeon.

Patrice lived across the street from a graveyard which added to the appeal for the scene girls. Many have lost their virginity in cemeteries; it was the perfect place aesthetically to help them get off. After showing Sheila his 2000s Emo vinyl collection, they went to the graveyard to stare at the tombstones. It was the perfect fake date. They stopped at an unmarked grave, the ground was dug up, and he pushed her in. Sheila just laid there. It was better than how she dreamed of dying, lying six feet under with dirt slowly being poured on her.

Patrice taxidermied all the pigeons he killed out of anger, so when he buried Sheila alive, he left his Sheila perched on the empty tombstone above the grave. He did this with all the scene girls he killed. When the FBI finally caught him, they stated that there were ten pigeons in the graveyard. And that when they connected them with police tape, it created a famous symbol in the community: two outward-facing trapezoids with a horizontal colon in the middle.

Karma caught up to him shortly after he started his stint in prison. He got HPV from one of his victims.

All of his taxidermied pigeons miss him dearly. They sit on their tombstones under a suburban sky and wait for his return.

Chapter Twenty-Five: The Eternal Wait

We have eternity.

We will stay perched

on these tombstones until

you die and reincarnate

as a maggot on the ground,

prime for a stomping.

We will watch

as your guts

explode outward;

as your feeble life

gets snuffed out like ours did.

We trusted you,

and now,

it's dead.

Chapter Twenty-Six: Life is Harde

Feedback from a microphone infiltrates the ears of listeners all over suburbia.

Roc clears his throat, "fellow scenesters. Today is a sadder day than usual. Sometimes the suffering we feel in our suburbia is too strong to handle."

"With no regret," Harde takes over the intro, "we have to inform our listeners that we will not be broadcasting our regular programs. To mourn a close friend who has selfishly taken his own life, we will be playing nothing but emotionally charged music."

"This will be the tenth day of silence in six months since we started this station."

"While we often joke about death (and on the surface, it may seem like the music we love glorifies and or makes light of it), we take this topic very seriously."

"The first song will be Hiding by Pianos Become the Teeth."

As both Roc and Harde exited the room, a faint sound of wooden chairs scraping the floor could be heard. They set up their broadcasts so that the songs play on a shuffle; it's just a Spotify playlist with over nine thousand songs.

No one else showed up to Brandon's entombment. His mom was no longer in the state; someone saw her hop on a bus to Atlantic City, and his sister had just gotten lost in the foster care system. So, only me, my co-host, and my mother, Julia, came to say our goodbyes.

I'm surprised my mother came with us. She had just gotten back from shooting her latest "movie" and saw us sneaking out the back of the house. Like all the other times we had to go to a funeral for a friend, she had the best timing to be an actual parent. My mother paid for his burial since none of his family came. After the second sendoff, she just up and bought a mausoleum.

Life is hard, and if you don't meet the expected result in your parents' eyes, then you're a fuckup. Of course, there are exceptions. However, when you grow up with the idea that money equals privilege (which has been repeated for centuries in your household), straying from the path means abandonment, both in life and death.

If I can take one thing away from my mother's kindness and acceptance of others, it is that family doesn't always mean blood ties. My mother isn't my real mother, and she loves me like her own. And my co-host is just a friend I met one day at a concert; however, he is my brother as well as my mother's second son.

Chapter Twenty-Seven: My Friend's Hot Mom

Even though I'm at a burial

I can't stop looking at my friend's hot mom.

A true giver.

Your light blonde hair,

blue eyes,

and 24-inch waist,

are objects of my faith.

Every time we bury a friend

I can't wait to see the features

that would even please the dead.

Am I a bad friend?

Chapter Twenty-Eight: Regrown Skin

I have finally felt the slight burning sensation you usually feel when walking out into the sun, or, at least, I think I did. After sitting in the dark for so long, my senses are jumbled.

Whoever stole my skin seems to have messed me up inside. Now, once a day, I shed it. Am I some sort of reptile?

Why was my skin harvested in the first place? It can't just be some surgeon who likes to think their god.

Will I see my skinner on 60 minutes, or will my case attract dust?

My sister couldn't handle our demonization. Thanks to whatever god actually watches over us, she's not dead, but she's no longer stable. Whenever she sees a sewing needle or hears the word needle, her body goes stiff.

Imagine walking past a television in a shop window and passing out because a news segment mentions the Space Needle. That hasn't actually happened, but you never know.

We're homeschooled now, not by choice, but by ostracization; parental enforcement. Like newborn lepers, we have been cut off from anything resembling the normalcy of old.

There isn't much to our lives now; I'm fixated on a monitor as we speak. Searching for answers on the internet (for a scenario that should only be possible in nightmares) is frustrating and stimulating. As for my sister, she took up drawing to try to recreate our attacker; her best attempt looks like a mutant meatball.

I have nothing more to say.

Chapter Twenty-Nine: The World Runs on Answers

How do you search for answers

to a question you don't know

how to articulate?

I type & type

but never get a result.

Turning off the safe search filter

doesn't make you an adult.

I click & click

changing my VPN;

hiding my failures.

Reality is short on saviours.

The world runs on answers,

and mine remain out of reach.

They're on vacation

at a faraway beach.

Chapter Thirty: Epilogue; The Short Reprieve in Suffering

Congratulations!

You have reached the end.

This is the short reprieve that is inherent in suffering.